This Little Tiger book belongs to:

_____

_____

_____

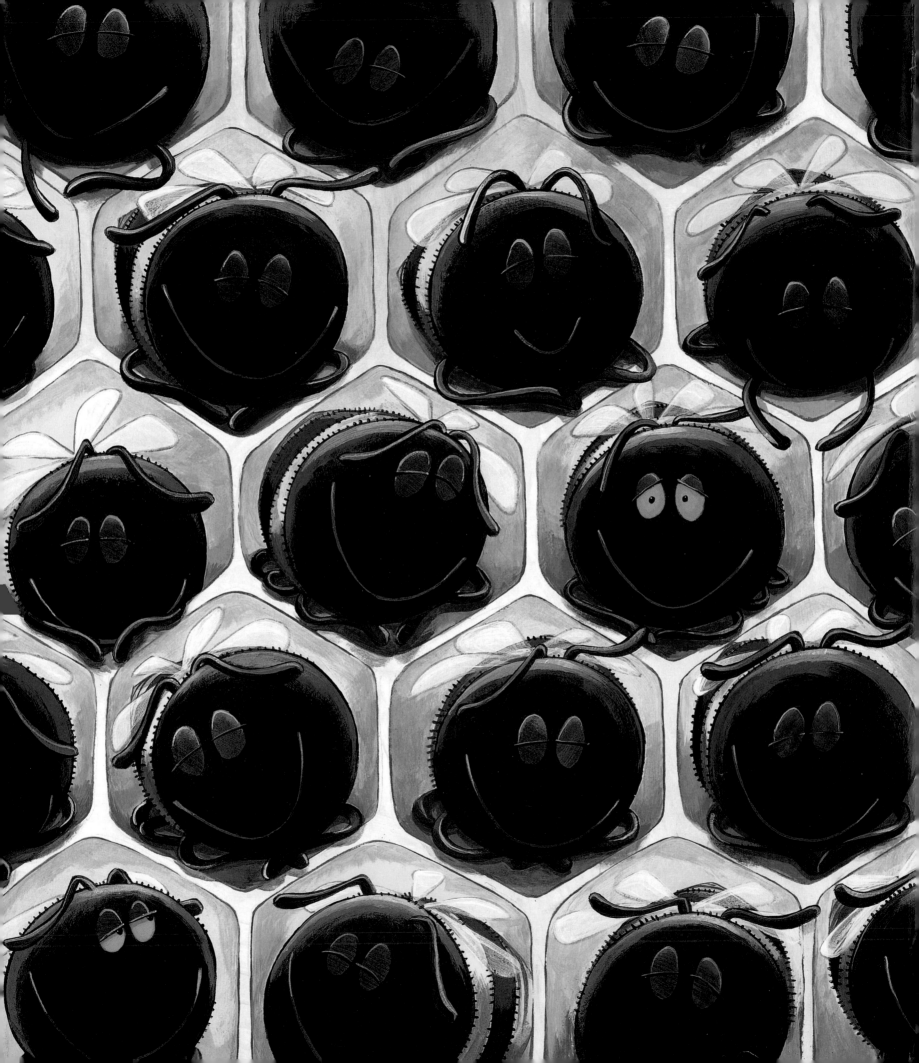

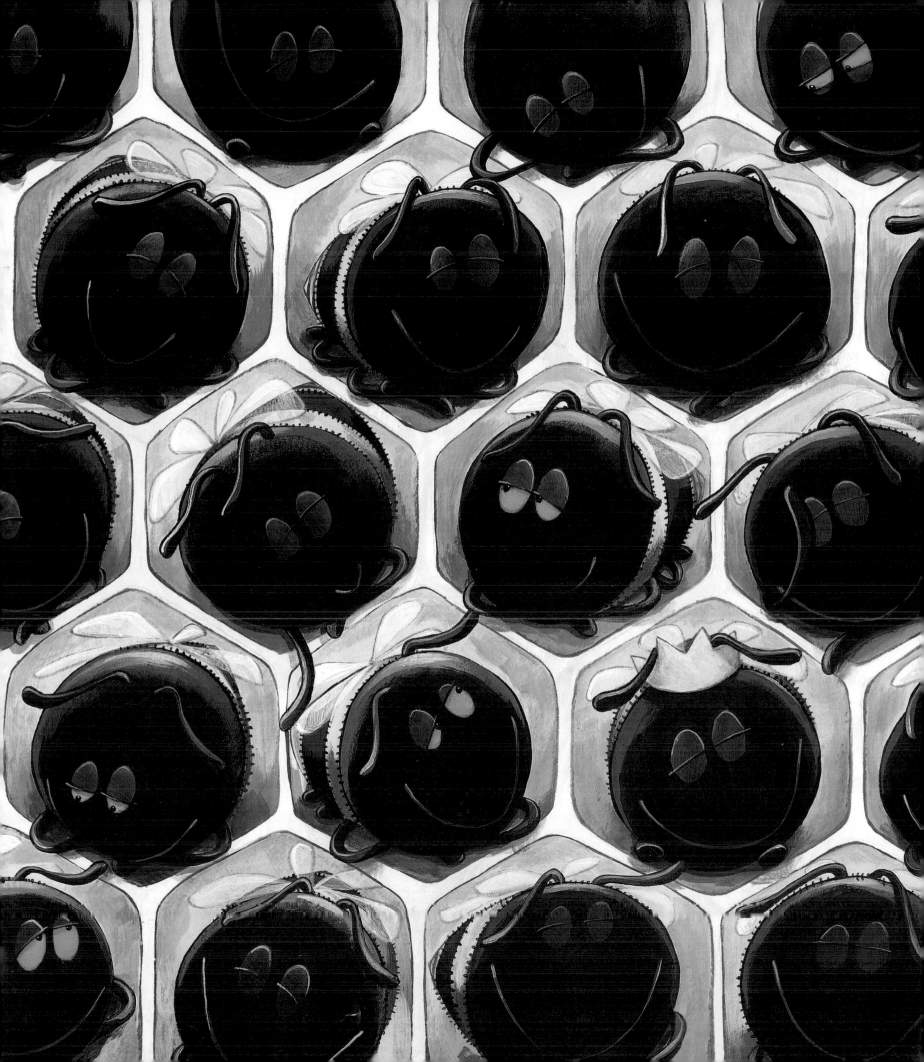

LITTLE TIGER PRESS LTD,
an imprint of the Little Tiger Group
1 Coda Studios, 189 Munster Road, London SW6 6AW
www.littletiger.co.uk
First published in Great Britain 2007 • This edition published 2018

CD contains:
1 - complete story with original music and sound effects
2 - story with page turn pings to encourage learner readers to join in

Running time over 15 mins
Produced by Stationhouse
Music composed by Sam Park
Story read by Justin Fletcher and Sophie Thompson
This recording copyright © Little Tiger Press 2012
℗ Sam Park

ISBN 978-1-78881-078-4
LTP/1900/2310/0418
Printed in China
10 9 8 7 6 5 4 3 2 1

FOR SAM, WHO TAUGHT ME
EVERYTHING I KNOW ABOUT BEES
~ S S

FOR MY BEEootiful
BaBEE, LEVI
~ J T

The Very Greedy Bee

Steve Smallman   Jack Tickle

LITTLE TIGER
LONDON

In a busy, buzzy beehive lived a very greedy bee. All the other bees worked hard making honey and cleaning the hive, but the Greedy Bee spent all day gobbling pollen and guzzling nectar.

SLURP! SLURP! BURP!

Eeek!

The Greedy Bee wouldn't share
his nectar with anyone.
He wouldn't even let a tired
ladybird sit on his flower.

"Find your own flower!" he
shouted. "This one is **MINE!**"

And when, one day, the Greedy Bee
found a meadow full of the biggest,
juiciest flowers he had ever seen,
he decided not to tell **ANYONE!**
    "**YUMMY!**" he buzzed. "Lots and
lots of flowers and they're all for **ME!**"

The Greedy Bee whizzed
and bizzed from flower
to flower, slurping and
burping, and growing
FATTER ...

and **FATTER** ...

and **FATTER**...

and **FATTER!**

At last his tummy was full and he settled down on a big pink flower in the warm yellow sunshine and fell fast asleep.

z z z z z z z !

When the Greedy Bee woke up,
it was **DARK**. He tried to fly,
but his tummy was so stodgy
and podgy that . . .

he went down instead
of up and landed,

BIFF!

BANG!

THUMP!

on the ground below.

"I'M SCARED!" cried the Greedy Bee,
"and I don't know how to get home!"
Then he saw two glowing eyes in the long grass.
"EEK!" he cried. "A MONSTER is coming to eat me!"

But it wasn't a monster, it was two friendly
fireflies, their bottoms glowing in the dark.
"What's wrong?" they asked.
"I'm too full to fly," wailed the Greedy Bee,
"and I can't walk home in the dark!"

"Follow us," said the fireflies, and they
all set off on the long, long journey home.

Through forests
of flowers and
squelchy mud . . .

over hills and under
hollows trudged the
Greedy Bee. He had
never walked so far
and he was very tired.

"Soon be there!" called the fireflies kindly.

Then they heard a whooshing, watery noise . . .

I'm almost home!" cried the Greedy
Bee excitedly. "It's the stream!"
	And it was, but his hive was on
the other side of it.

"Oh dear," cried the Greedy Bee, flopping down with a flump on the floor. "How will I ever get across?" he sniffled sadly.

"We'll help you!" said a tiny ant with a big leaf.

The ant and his friends flipped
one of their leaves into the water.
"Jump in!" they cried.
Then, helped by the fireflies,
the Greedy Bee and the ants
made their way, splishing
and splashing, over to the
other side of the stream.

"**HOORAY, I'M HOME!**" cried the Greedy Bee. "Wherever have you been?" called the other bees. "**I OVERSLURPED!**" said the Greedy Bee. "I would never have got home if my new friends hadn't been so kind, so now I'm going to share my best honey with them. Would you like some too?"

"Great!" said the other bees. "Let's have a party!"

Everyone tucked
into a midnight feast of
yummy, runny honey.
All except for one **VERY**
sleepy, **VERY** happy,
but **NOT** so greedy bee!

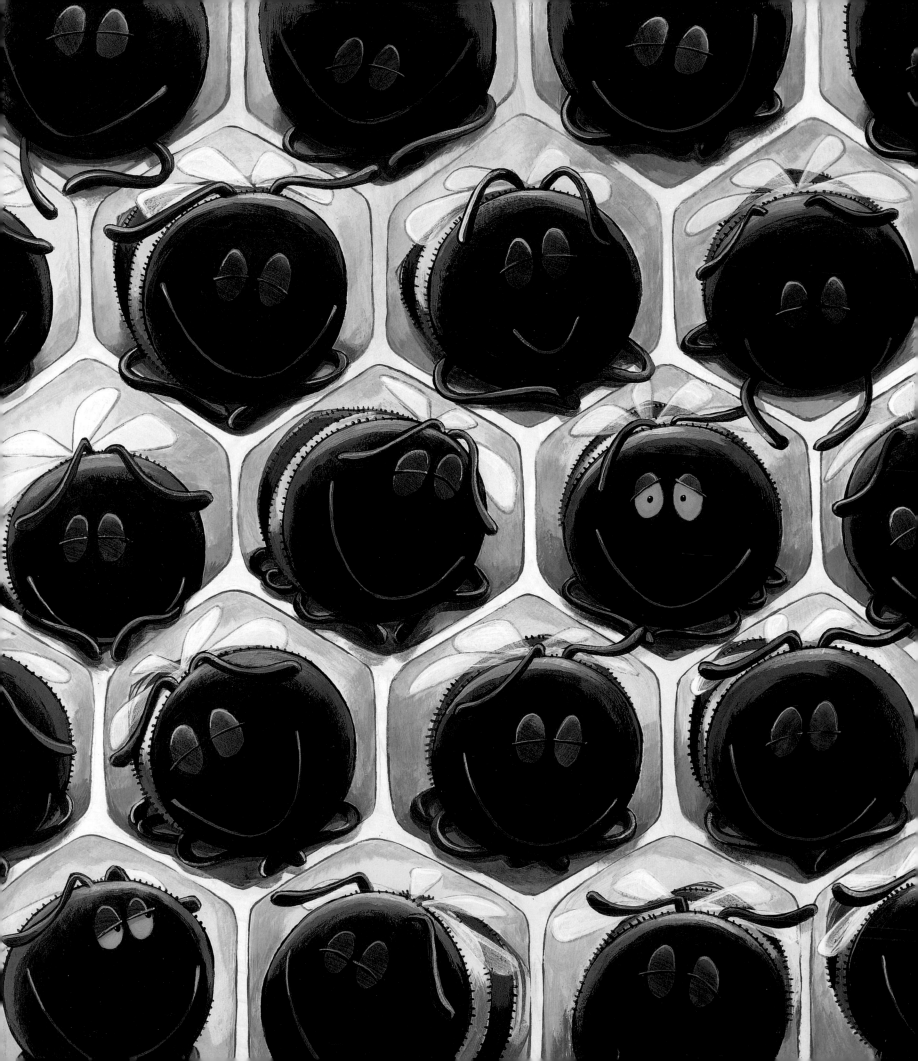

More fabulous books
from Little Tiger Press!

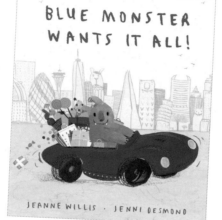

For information regarding any of the above books or for our catalogue, please contact us:
Little Tiger Press, 1 Coda Studios, 189 Munster Road, London SW6 6AW
Tel: 020 7385 6333 • E-mail: contact@littletiger.co.uk • www.littletiger.co.uk